GOD'S BLACK COLORS

BY

BETTINA JONES

Published in the United States of America

ISBN 978-1-955243-66-7 (SC)
ISBN 978-1-955243-67-4 (HC)
ISBN 978-1-955243-68-1 (Ebook)

Bettina Jones
1968 S. Coast Hwy # 3880
Laguna Beach, CA 92651
www.stellarliterary.com

Order Information and Rights Permission:

Quantity sales. Special discounts might be available on quantity purchases by corporations, associations, and others. For details, contact the publisher at the address above.

For Book Rights Adaptation and other Rights Permission. Call us at toll-free 1-888-945-8513 or send us an email at admin@stellarliterary.com.

Hi my name is Selena and I'm 6 years old. My favorite color in the world is purple. This is what I look like…..

I even wear purple glasses sometimes!!

I also have a three year old brother named Jase. He likes to ru
and jump all the time. His favorite color is blue, he wears it a
the time.

We play together when I get home from school everyday. Ou
favorite games to play are kickball with the other neighborhoo
kids and card games with each other.

Jase and I also love watching television and eating popcor
together.

We also have a dog named Lily. She is a huge dog. She is a dalmation, she is all white with black spots. She lives in the house with our family and can run really fast. Sometimes Jase and I will lay on her like a pillow as we watch television.

Lily has her own room with a bed and an area for food and water. Most of the time she sleeps in my room on the floor. I really love Lily and enjoy playing with her. I'm so happy we have her.

We also have a very big back yard, that Lily likes to run fast back and forth in. Jase and I throw toys for her to catch in her mouth, she loves this game. We also run with her and let her chase us up and down the yard for hours. Before we go in the house we put everything away and Lily drinks a lot of water.

My mommy and daddy are really great parents to Jase and I. My mommy is an artist and my daddy is a mechanic. They work very hard everyday to make a happy home for all of us. They always do fun things with us.

One time we all went to the Beach and we had so much fun because we got to swim and see a real dolphin.

We also get to go to the movies sometimes and get to eat movie popcorn and snacks while watching a new movie. These are always exciting family times.

They also read us bedtime stories at night before we go to bed. My favorite bedtime stories are the ones about mermaids and fairies. Jase said his favorite stories are the ones about superheroes. They give us lots of love and care.

My grandmother visits our family every year for the summer. She always brings me more purple gifts I like. One time she brought me a real nice purple coat for the winter so I can always be warm.

Then another time she got me a cool purple watch so I can know the time. I wear it on my left wrist.

Also one time she got to come in the winter time and she brought me a purple sweater with leggings and some purple earrings to match.

I was so happy, I gave her the biggest hug.

My neighborhood is very close to my school, so I can walk hom everyday from school. Sometimes when I walk home, I preten I'm on an adventure like in my bedtime stories.

When I get home from school my mommy always has a deliciou snack for me. I have to do my homework before I get to watc television with Jase and Lily. I really do not like homework. I wis teachers would stop giving homework, especially Math.

Our house is green and is in the middle of two other houses. Th other two houses do not have kids living in them or dogs. Ther is a cat that lives in the third house next to ours named Zoe. Sh is all gray and follows me home from school sometimes, she is nice cat.

Sometimes Zoe is a part of my pretend adventures on my way home. I pretend I am a witch and she is my cat. We go around making things glitter and sparkle with my magic wand. I always make myself a good witch and do good things for everyone.

Zoe and I fly on my broomstick through the imaginary town I created with my magic wand. It's called Star Land and there are mermaids, fairies and flowers that talk. I made them all sparkly with my wand and most of them are some sort of purple color.

I made my magic wand out of a stick I found in my yard. I put some glue on one end of it and sprinkled purple glitter on it. I tied a shoelace under the glitter part for the handle. My mommy helped me so I didn't get glitter all over the floor.

One time after school it was raining, I pretended that the flower in Star Land needed me to help them from melting. The fairie couldn't help because they couldn't fly in the rain and use thei magic. And the mermaids couldn't come out of the water to hel so it was up to me and Zoe.

So I got to my neighborhood and saw Zoe waiting for me with her magic cape. She said hurry the flowers need us, they nee you to wave your magic wand over them. I reached in m backpack and pulled out my wand, we started running toward the flowers.

As Zoe and I ran a gust of wind hit a puddle and it came towar us, I waved my wand at the water, then it went in anothe direction. We kept on running feeling very happy that we jus dodged being splashed.

We finally got to the flowers and I waved my magic wand ove them so they could stop melting. All of a sudden the rain go lighter and the flowers began to sit up again. Zoe started to chee and said, "we did it". Zoe cape disappeared, I put my wand up then continued walking home.

have a few favorite things I like to do when I get home after school and on the weekends. One of the things I like to do is color in my coloring books with Jase. We'll color for hours and then show our mommy so she can put them up on the front of the fridge.

I also like to go roller skating at the skate rink. I like the music they play when I'm skating. My daddy bought me some white skates with purple writing on them and pom poms. Sometimes when I can't go to the skating rink, I skate on the streets in my neighborhood.

Another favorite thing I like to do is to write in my journal at school in the morning. When I first get to school everyday we have "Journal Time" and my teacher writes a theme on the board that the class has to write about and I always make my stories real interesting, exciting and draw pictures to help describe what I am writing about.

My teacher said the stories I write are very creative and sh
always gives me a good grade. One time she asked me, could sh
submit one of my stories for the school writing contest becaus
she thought I could win. I told her she could and I won first plac

The first place prize was a pizza party for the whole class an
free tickets to the roller rink. I was so happy. The pizza party wa
so much fun and my mommy got to come too. Everyone was s
happy that I had won the contest mainly because we got to ea
pizza and also cupcakes. Our class also got to watch movies an
play some games outdoors, it was a fun day at school.

When I got home, my mommy made my favorite dinne
spaghetti. Then my daddy and Jase brought me some flowers fc
winning the contest. The flowers were called roses and the
were all different colors, and they were all pretty.

Even though my class was happy for me winning the writing contest, I do not have a lot of friends. Kids at school talk about me but I still call them my friends. I really want them to be my friends and not make fun of me.

One time I brought my favorite book for storytime and during recess, someone stole my book. I was so sad and hurt. Some of the kids laughed at me because I could not find my book. My teacher said she looked for it but was not able to find it.

My "friends" at school also ask me why my skin so light and my eyes slant but I say I'm black? They say I can't be black and look like me. They say I'm white and Chinese but not black. I say to them that my mommy and daddy are both black people so that makes me black but they don't believe me and laugh. I cry when I'm by myself.

I often eat lunch by myself. My 'friends" at school throw food in my hair and clothes and call me names. They also push me in line as we walk to and from the cafeteria. They constantly make fun of how I look and tell me I'm not black. I cry again.

My teacher notices me crying and tells my mommy how the other kids have been treating me. My mommy tells me that I can't help how I look and that I am pretty. I still look in the mirror wishing my skin was darker so that I could be accepted as a black girl and pretty.

I go to school everyday and notice so many different kinds of black girls.

see Ava and she light but like a caramel color and she black. Her color make me think of that stuff they put on the top of ice ream to make it taste more yummy. Ava is nice to me and she an sing like a bird.

Then there's Reina, she can draw really well, Both her parent
are from Africa. She is dark skinned, her skin looks like chocolat
to me. I think she is beautiful. She is also very good at math. Sh
is older than me, she is 8 years old and really smart.

also see Melody and she is lighter than me. She got blue eyes and dark blonde hair. She say she black too because her daddy black but her mommy is white. Melody likes to play kickball and soccer.

Lastly, I always see Briana, she is in my class. She is lighter than me and Melody. She told me she is called an Albino and she is black too, like me. I think to myself, now I'm even more confused.

went home and talked to my mommy again because I feel so onfused about how everybody black but they look different. lso, why do kids make fun of how my "black" looks?

Iy mommy tells me again that I cannot help how I look and that am pretty. She also tells me to ignore the kids that are picking n me. I say okay, mommy and go to my room for bedtime.

After I say my prayers and lay down to go to bed, I still wonder how all of us are black but come in different colors. I think what else is made like that…..Hmmmmm…….I think………. I think……..

Oh yea!! I got it!!! A Rose!!!!!

I sit up in my bed and count on my small fingers, there's a red rose, a yellow rose, a pink rose and white rose, etc. and yet they are all flowers, actually the same flower just different colors and beautiful.

Just like us, we are all God's Black Colors and Beautiful.